OAK LAWN PUBLIC LIBRARY
3 1186 00749 1095
P9-CFD-740

STR

To Scott
—D. C.

For my mother and father
—S. M.

Atheneum Books for Young Readers • An imprint of Simon & Schuster Children's Publishing Division • 1230 Avenue of the Americas • New York, New York 10020 • • Book design by Ann Bobco and Sonia Chaghatzbanian • The text for this book is set in Bliss. • The illustrations for this book are rendered in pen and ink with digital color. • Manufactured in China • First Edition • 10 9 8 7 6 5 4 3 2 1 • Library of Congress Cataloging-in-Publication Data • Cronin, Doreen. • Stretch / Doreen Cronin ; illustrated by Scott Menchin.—1st ed. • p. cm. • Summary: Rhyming text describes the many ways to stretch. • ISBN: 978-1-4169-5341-8 • [1. Stories in rhyme. 2. Stretching exercises—Fiction.] I. Menchin, Scott, ill. II. Title. • PZ8.3.C879Str 2009 • [E]—dc22 • 2007044476

etch

doreen cronin

and scott menchin

atheneum books for young readers new york • london • toronto • sydney

Stretch with me,
hands in the air!
Count to three. . . .

Hold it right there!

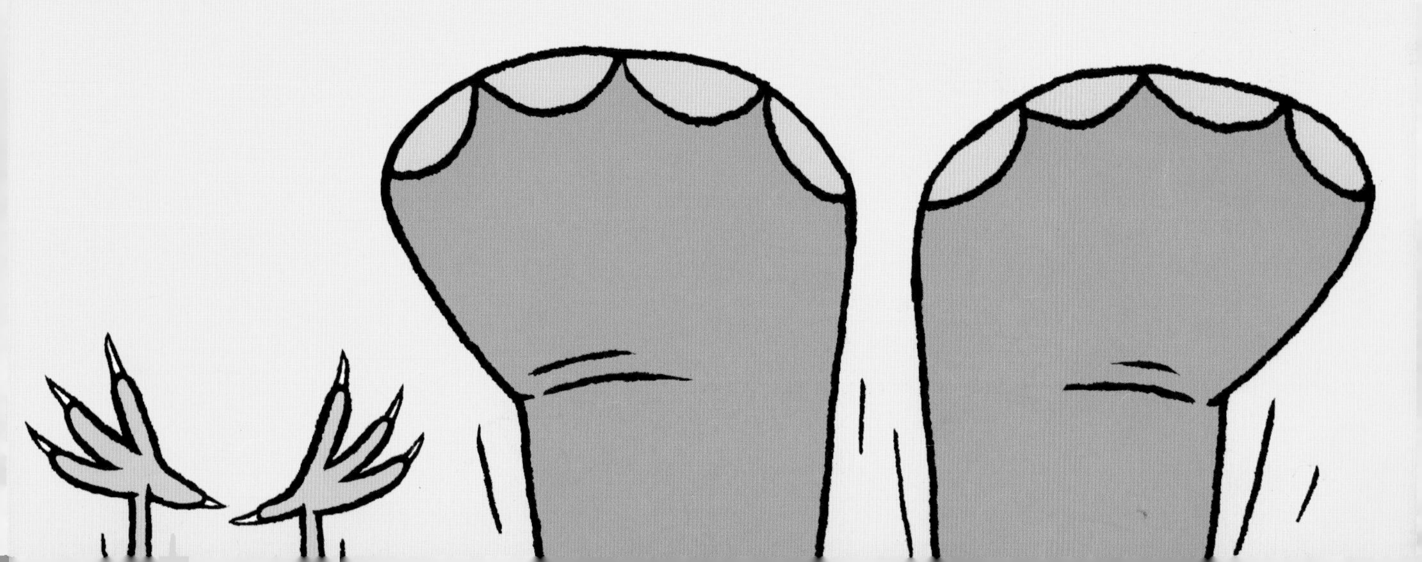

Stretch up **high** for a snack in the trees.

Stretch out wide

for a ride on the breeze.

Can you stretch to the ceiling?

Can you **stretch** to the floor?

You can stretch with a whisper,

you
can
stretch
with
a
roar.

I can **stretch** underwater,

I can **stretch** on a wave.

I can stretch on a surfboard

if I'm very, very

brave.

Some
will
stretch
to show you
feathers.

Some will stretch
to show you
spots.

A **stretch** that goes a **stretch** too far

might
tie
you
up
in
knots.

A yawn is just a stretch

that starts down deep inside.

It travels up into
your mouth
and makes
it open
wide.

If I were an inchworm, I'd **stretch**

from place to place.

If I were an astronaut,

I'd stretch in outer space.

I stretch my lungs to take
a breath,

then blow out

nice

and

s l o w.

A bubble will stretch and **stretch**. . .

until there's **no** room left to **grow.**

POP!

If you stretch me

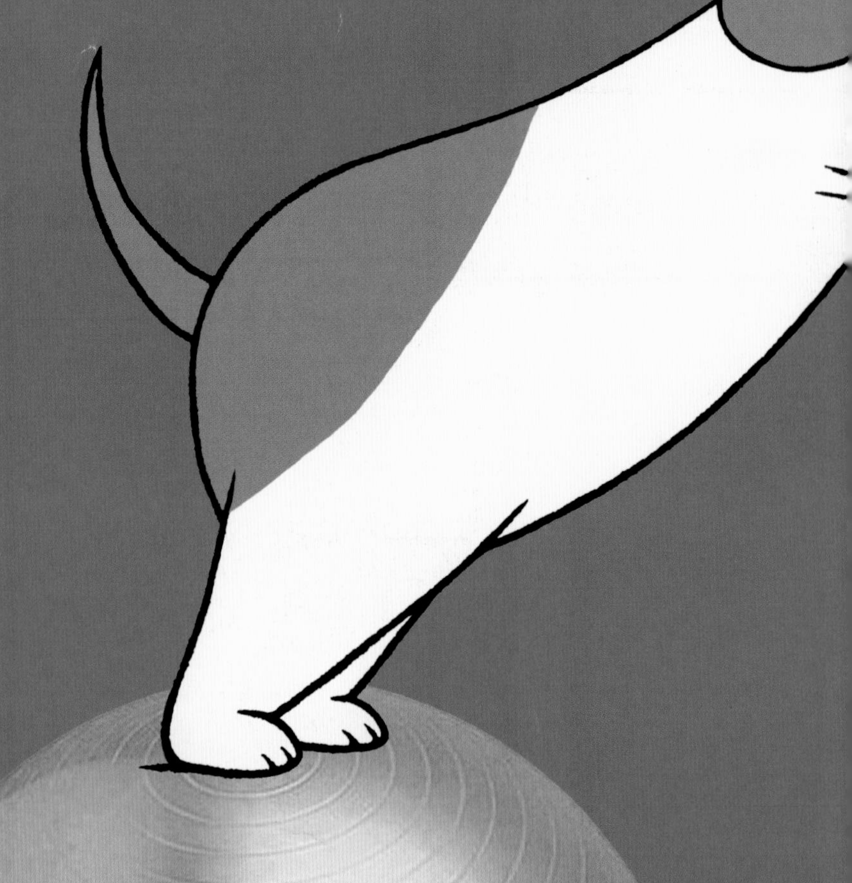

and I stretch you . . .

we'll stretch twice as far. . . .

Who
knows
what
we
can
do?